KEVIN'S Great ESCAPE

BY THE REMARKABLE DOUBLE ACT THAT IS

PHILIP REEVE AND SARAH McINTYRE

OXFORD
UNIVERSITY PRESS

This is Kevin, the roly-poly flying pony.

And this is Max,

who is Kevin's best friend.

This is the block of flats where Max
and Kevin live. That's Max's family's
flat on the top floor. Kevin has a nest
on the roof.

BISCUITS OUT

DEDICATED TO THESE TWO SUPERSTARS

ARETHA

CHARIS

OXFORD
UNIVERSITY PRESS

Great Clarendon Street, Oxford OX2 6DP
Oxford University Press is a department of the University of Oxford.
It furthers the University's objective of excellence in research, scholarship,
and education by publishing worldwide. Oxford is a registered trade mark
of Oxford University Press in the UK and in certain other countries

Database right Oxford University Press (maker)

First published 2019

British Library Cataloguing in Publication Data

Data available

ISBN: 978-0-19-276611-3

1 3 5 7 9 10 8 6 4 2

Printed in China

Paper used in the production of this book is a natural,
recyclable product made from wood grown in sustainable forests.
The manufacturing process conforms to the environmental
regulations of the country of origin.

This is the town of Bumbleford. It's an ordinary sort of town, except that it's not so very far from the wild, wet hills of the Outermost West, where some of the strange creatures out of legends and fairy tales still live. (The wild, wet hills are where Kevin blew in from.)

And this is Nobbly Nora, a friendly tortoise. (She doesn't have anything to do with this story at all, she just wanted to be in a book.)

AND NOW, CHAPTER ONE →

ONE

MISTY TWIGLET'S BIGGEST FAN

One afternoon, right at the beginning of the autumn half-term holidays, Kevin was happily nibbling hay on his rooftop when he was startled by a loud shout or scream from somewhere below.

'AAAAAAAAH!'

it went.

Kevin looked over at the pigeons dozing

in their coop on the other side of the
roof. That, he thought to himself, was a
loud shout, or scream. It probably means
someone is in TROUBLE. He fluffed
up his wings importantly. 'This sounds
like a job for KEVIN, the ROLY-POLY
FLYING PONY.'

'Show off!' muttered the pigeons, as
Kevin flapped up into the air. But they
were just jealous because they were shut
in their coop and couldn't go for a proper
fly until their human, Gordon, came to
let them out. Kevin could come and go
whenever he wanted.

'AAAAH! AAAAH! AAAAH!' went the
screams. They seemed to be coming from
inside Max's family's flat. Kevin landed
on the balcony outside the living room

and poked his head in through the open window to see what the matter was.

Daisy, Max's sister, was jumping up and down and pointing at the TV.

'Oh Emm Geee!' she screeched. 'Misty Twiglet is moving to Bumbleford! Misty Twiglet is moving to Bumbleford!' She was so excited that she started getting all her words muddled up. 'Movey Bumlet is twiggling to Mistyford!'

Kevin watched in an interested sort of way as Max and his mum and dad came hurrying in to see what all the fuss was about. Daisy said, 'Twiggley Bum-mist is . . . Musty . . . Fumble . . . bum . . . Oh, just LOOK!' And she turned up the volume on the TV so they could all hear the news report that had got her so worked up.

'Spooky pop sensation Misty Twiglet has bought Gloomsbury Grange near Bumbleford,' the reporter was saying. 'The house will be Misty's country retreat when she isn't busy recording albums or playing concerts in packed stadiums. She's sure to get lots of ideas for new songs while wandering around the old house and its enormous, wooded grounds.'

'She might come to do her shopping in Bumbleford!' said Daisy.

'She might get her hair done at Mum's salon!'

'Ooh, I don't think I've ever done a haircut for a pop sensation before,' said Mum.

'I thought you were mainly doing mermaids' hair now,' said Max. 'The salon is full of water.

I don't think Misty Twiglet could hold her breath long enough to get a proper haircut there.'

'I bet she could,' said Daisy. 'Misty's a brilliant singer, so she has highly trained lungs. Or she could come here to the flat to get her hair cut! Misty can do ANYTHING SHE WANTS TO.'

'But she probably wouldn't want to come shopping in Bumbleford,' Dad pointed out. 'She's a spooky pop sensation. Spooky pop sensations don't go shopping. They have other people to go shopping for them.'

'But not for haircuts,' said Daisy. 'They don't have other people to get haircuts for them. That would be silly.'

Kevin was confused. He knew a lot more words than most ponies did, but he wasn't sure what a 'pop sensation' was. He wondered if it was something like the fizzy, sneezy sort of feeling he had got that time he tried drinking some of Max's cola.

Max came out on to the balcony to explain things to him. 'Misty Twiglet is Daisy's favourite pop star,' he said. 'She dresses up like a posh cobweb and sings gloomy songs about ghosts and haunted wardrobes. All her videos are filmed in foggy graveyards, and all her songs go something like, "Ooooh I'm so miserable oooh ooooh I'm stuck in this haunted wardrobe". Daisy is her BIGGEST FAN. She dresses like Misty, she's covered her room in posters of Misty, she listens to Misty's songs ALL THE TIME.'

'Oh,' said Kevin. That explained the strange wailing noises he had heard coming from Daisy's room.

'I bet she wants to BE Misty

Twiglet,' said Max.

'I do not!' said Daisy, overhearing. 'I just happen to think Misty's really cool and super-talented and a wonderful person, that's all.'

'You wish Misty Twiglet was your big sister!' said Max.

'I'd rather have someone COOL and SUPER-TALENTED like Misty Twiglet for a big sister than someone STUPID and ANNOYING for a little brother,' said Daisy.

'Now then kids,' warned Dad, 'Let's not have an argument.'

'Anyway,' said Mum, 'Gloomsbury Grange is miles from here. I don't think Misty Twiglet is likely to show up in Bumbleford, and even if she does, I don't think she'll be calling on us.'

Just then—DING-DONG!—the doorbell rang.

TWO

BAZ GUMPTION

Kevin, Max and Daisy all peered over the balcony railing. There below them, parked outside the front of the flats, was the flashiest, shiniest, sports car they had ever seen.

'Maybe it's Misty Twiglet!' whispered Daisy.

'It can't be,' said Dad.

'Let's go and find out!' shouted Max.

'Do be careful, Max,' Mum warned, as

he leaped up onto Kevin's back and Kevin jumped off the balcony and went flapping down to land beside the sleek blue car, startling the person who was stepping out of it.

The person wasn't Misty Twiglet. It was a man in a shiny jacket and shiny dark glasses, and once he had got over the shock of having a roly-poly flying pony land beside him, he smiled a shiny smile and held out a small white card to Max.

'You're just the dude I want to see!' he said.

Max looked at the card. It said,

BAZ GUMPTION,
SUPERSTAR TALENT
MANAGEMENT

'I work for Misty Twiglet,' Baz Gumption explained. 'You may know her hit songs *Vampire Disco* and *Trapped (In a Haunted Wardrobe)*. She just bought a big house in these parts . . .'

'Yes, we saw it on the telly,' said Max.

The front door of the flats banged opened and Daisy came running out with Mum and Dad close behind her—they'd come down in the lift to see what was going on.

'This is my mum and dad and my sister,' said Max. 'Mum, Dad, this is . . .'

'It's BAZ GUMPTION!' said Daisy. 'He's Misty's manager! He sets up all her million-dollar music deals!'

'That's right, little dudette,' said Baz, swinging his shiny smile towards her like a dazzling desk lamp. 'And now I'm here to do a deal with you! Misty's new place has a HUGE garden—acres of land—and she's asked me to find some interesting animals to live in it. And what could be more interesting than a real, live, flying pony?

As soon as I heard about yours I knew he'd be just the thing. How much do you want for him?'

'Nothing!' said Max. 'I mean . . .'

'Kevin's not for sale!' said Mum.

'He's our friend,' said Daisy.

'Oh, sure,' said Baz Gumption. 'But your friend would be way better off living in Misty Twiglet's garden than up on your roof.'

'He doesn't always live on the roof,' said Max. 'He can fly off whenever he wants to his nest in the wild, wet hills. But he always comes back.'

'He can make a nest in Misty's new garden,' said Baz Gumption. 'There are hundreds of trees to choose from, and he'll have loads of space, a state-of-the-art stable, all the food he can eat . . .'

Kevin pricked up his ears at that. 'Biscuits?' he asked.

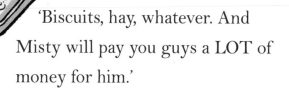

'Biscuits, hay, whatever. And Misty will pay you guys a LOT of money for him.'

Max and his family all shook their heads. 'He's NOT for sale,' Mum said firmly. 'We don't OWN Kevin. He's our friend, and he goes where he chooses.'

Baz Gumption sighed. 'Well, why don't you all come and visit Misty at her new place anyway? Have a look around? Then Kenneth can see for himself how happy he'd be there.'

'It's KEVIN,' neighed Kevin, and he snuggled up close to Max to show that he was quite happy living on Max's roof and didn't want to move to

Misty Twiglet's place even if there WERE biscuits there.

'Well, I suppose if it was just for a visit . . .' said Daisy hopefully, going all dreamy-eyed at the thought of actually meeting her idol.

'Drop by any time!' said Baz. 'Well, make it today—Misty is off to the big city tonight. She's recording a charity single to raise awareness about Athlete's Foot.'

'What's Athlete's Foot?' asked Max.

Baz looked solemnly at him. 'That, my dude, is exactly why we need to raise awareness about it.'

'We could just drop in, couldn't we?' Daisy asked her parents hopefully. 'It wouldn't do any harm just to go and look.'

'Sorry, Daisy, but we can't,' said Mum,

who had decided that she didn't trust Baz Gumption and his shiny smiles one little bit. 'Max has his swimming competition this evening, remember? So thank you, Mr Gumption, but we are definitely NOT interested.'

Baz Gumption scowled while trying to keep smiling, which was an interesting look. 'No worries!' he said. 'If you change your mind you can just give me a call—my number is on the back of the card.'

Then he got back into his shiny car, its engine growled like a peckish puma, and it drove away.

'Well!' said Mum.

'Well!' said Dad.

'We could just have gone to *look* . . .' sulked Daisy.

'Kevin is NOT FOR SALE,' said Max.

'Biscuits?' said Kevin, who had just realized that it was the end of Chapter Two already and he hadn't had any custard creams yet.

So they all went back upstairs for a snack.

THREE

GLOOMSBURY GRANGE

At 5 o'clock that evening Max had to be at
Bumbleford Swimming Pool to take part
in the swimming competition. Mum and
Dad went along to watch, but Daisy stayed
at home, and so did Kevin, because Kevin

wasn't allowed in the swimming pool—not after what happened last time . . .

He sat in his nest on the roof, thinking happy thoughts about custard creams and all the fun things he was going to do with Max and Daisy in the school holidays.

Downstairs, Daisy sat in her room, listening to her favourite Misty Twiglet album, *Sad Songs from Gloomy Graveyards.* She had rescued Baz Gumption's business card from the recycling bin where Max had chucked it, and from time to time she looked at it and sighed a wistful sigh. It seemed so unfair! Misty Twiglet, who Daisy wanted to meet more than ANYONE ELSE IN THE WORLD had ACTUALLY INVITED DAISY TO HER HOUSE and she wasn't allowed to go! And she was sure that Misty would love to meet Kevin, and she'd be certain to understand that he was Max and Daisy's friend and couldn't go to live at Gloomsbury Grange. Misty Twiglet was famous for being kind to animals—Daisy had read on the Official Misty Twiglet Fan

Page how the spooky pop sensation had once rescued a bat which had got stuck in her washing machine.

'What harm could it do?' Daisy asked herself. (She meant what harm could going to see Misty Twiglet do, not the bat-in-the-washing-machine thing, that was obviously a really dangerous place for a bat, even one that needed a wash.)

As the album came to an end, Daisy made a big decision. She went out of the flat and climbed the stairs to the roof. 'Kevin,' she said, 'I'm bored. How about taking me for a fly?'

Kevin wasn't sure. He was feeling a bit sleepy, and Daisy was heavier than Max. 'Where to?' he asked.

'I thought we could go to Misty

Twiglet's new house. Just to say hello . . .'

'Biscuits!' neighed Kevin. He hadn't completely understood the conversation with Baz Gumption earlier, but he had definitely got the impression that Misty Twiglet was famous and important and had biscuits, and he was interested to find out what sort of biscuits a famous and important person would have.

'Oh, there'll be loads of biscuits!' said Daisy.

'Custard creams?' asked Kevin.

'Triple-decker ones, with sprinkles,' Daisy promised.

Kevin hopped out of his nest and gave his wings a couple of quick flaps to limber up. Then Daisy climbed onto his back and they took off together into the evening sky.

Daisy had a route-finding app on her
phone, so it wasn't hard to find the way to
Gloomsbury Grange. The old house stood
about half an hour's pony flight outside
Bumbleford, on the edge of a village called
Little Strimming. Its huge, overgrown
grounds were ringed by a high stone wall.
As Kevin swooped over the wall and flew
down towards the house Daisy saw the
glitter of a lake among the woods below,
and a lawn dotted with statues. At the
front of the house the sleek sports car
from earlier was parked next to a long

black car. It was all Very Impressive.

Kevin landed beside the cars. Daisy scrambled down, smoothed her wind-blown hair, and walked up the steps to the black front door with Kevin trotting behind her. There was a big silver door knocker in the shape of a snake eating its own tail. 'Stupid snake!' said Kevin. You'd never catch a flying pony doing something as stupid as eating his own tail, he thought. Then he wondered what his tail tasted like and turned round to have a nibble.

Daisy lifted the knocker and let it fall against the thick, dark oak of the door. **BOOM!** it went, and she imagined the sound echoing along the dark corridors of the old house, shaking deathwatch beetles out of the wood panelling and waking the ghosts who probably haunted the place. She reminded herself that she wasn't scared of ghosts. She loved darkness and spooky old houses. Even so, she could not help wondering if this had really been a good idea. 'Perhaps we should just go home,' she started to say, but she had only got as far as, 'Perhaps–' when the door swung open.

Daisy found herself face to face with an enormous man. Actually, it was more like

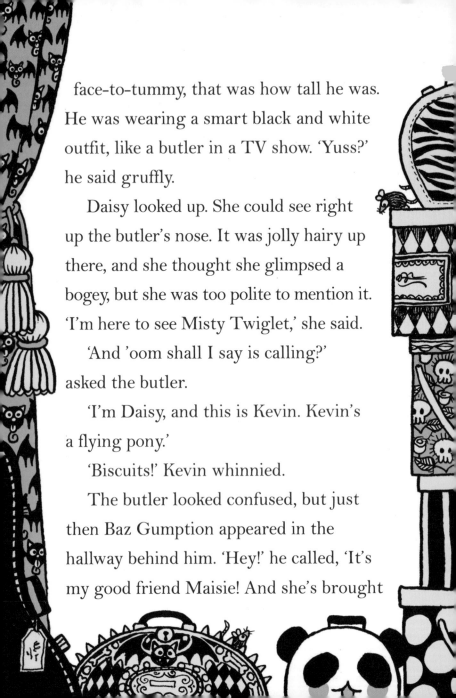

face-to-tummy, that was how tall he was.
He was wearing a smart black and white
outfit, like a butler in a TV show. 'Yuss?'
he said gruffly.

Daisy looked up. She could see right
up the butler's nose. It was jolly hairy up
there, and she thought she glimpsed a
bogey, but she was too polite to mention it.
'I'm here to see Misty Twiglet,' she said.

'And 'oom shall I say is calling?'
asked the butler.

'I'm Daisy, and this is Kevin. Kevin's
a flying pony.'

'Biscuits!' Kevin whinnied.

The butler looked confused, but just
then Baz Gumption appeared in the
hallway behind him. 'Hey!' he called, 'It's
my good friend Maisie! And she's brought

Kenneth with her!'

'Daisy,' said Daisy.

'Kevin,' said Kevin.

'You can let them in, Lumphammer,' Baz told the butler. 'They're just in time to see Misty before she leaves.'

The butler stood aside, and Daisy and Kevin went past him into the house. It was gigantic. Most houses were a bit of a tight squeeze for Kevin and he was always worried about knocking ornaments off shelves with his wings, but in Gloomsbury Grange there was plenty of room for him, and the ornaments were things like suits of armour which weren't easy to knock over. In the middle of the hall was a big heap of suitcases and hatboxes.

'This is Misty's luggage for her trip to

the big city,' said Baz, leading Daisy and
Kevin past the teetering stack.

'How long will she be away for?'
asked Daisy.

'Just an overnight trip. She'll
be back this time tomorrow.'

Baz opened a big door and
showed the visitors into another
enormous room. 'Misty!' he
shouted. 'Someone to see you!'

Daisy and Kevin walked
into the room. It seemed to
be empty. Not completely, of
course—there were sofas and
tables and pot plants and book
cases and pictures and a TV
the size of the main screen at
Bumbleford Cinema, but there

was no sign of a spooky pop sensation.
Daisy was just starting to wonder if Baz
Gumption was playing a practical joke
on her when a section of panelling
next to the fireplace swung open and
Misty Twiglet herself stepped out.
She was much smaller than she
looked in pictures and videos, but
just as lovely.

'Wow!' Misty said. 'This house is SO
COOL!' She didn't seem surprised to find
Daisy standing staring at her. 'It's got
a SECRET PASSAGE!' she explained.
'When I was little I always wanted to live
in a house with an actual secret passage.
I can't wait to move in properly! Baz has
been here for a few weeks getting things
ready, but I've been so busy, this is the first

chance I've really had to look around. Oh, hey, what an adorable little flying pony!' She ran lightly to where Kevin stood, and kissed him on the nose. 'You must be Kevin! Baz has been telling me all about you!'

Kevin didn't say anything. He had never been kissed on the nose by a pop sensation before, and he was a bit overwhelmed.

Daisy didn't say anything either. She had all sorts of questions she wanted to ask, like, 'Where do you get your ideas from?' and 'How did a bat get into your washing machine?', but her mouth had gone all shy and she could only stand and stare at Misty Twiglet. When Misty turned to her and said, 'So you must be Daisy?' she wondered if she should explain that she preferred to be called ELVIRA because it sounded so much more mysterious, but all she could manage to say was, 'Mnk, grmmple, pffff!'

'Thanks so much for bringing Kevin!' the pop star said. 'Hey, Baz, have I got time to chat to Daisy before I go? Fetch some cakes and things.' As Baz left, she sat down on a black sofa and patted the cushion beside her to show that Daisy should sit next to her. 'I've been reading about Kevin on the internet,' she said. 'He was so brave when you had that awful flood! And is it true your mum's a hairdresser for mermaids? I love it round here, all these strange creatures you have! We don't have any mermaids or flying ponies in the big city.'

'I—I really like your music!' said Daisy, in a tiny, shy voice.

Misty smiled. 'Which of my albums is your favourite?'

'*Sad Songs from Gloomy Graveyards,*' said Daisy.

She must have said the wrong thing. Misty kept smiling, but the smile turned a bit sad around the edges. 'That was my first one,' she sighed. 'That's the one everyone likes.'

'The others are good, too!' said Daisy quickly.

'But not AS good,' said Misty. 'People are getting tired of my stuff, I know. Even I'm getting tired of it. I wish I could find a new sound. But hey, maybe Kevin here will inspire me.'

'Me?' said Kevin. He didn't really know anything about music, but he wanted to be helpful, so he started humming. 'Pom pomm pa-pomm . . .'

Luckily Baz Gumption came back just then, and even more luckily he was carrying a tray of cakes, plates, glasses, and three different types of juice. Kevin was a bit disappointed to see that there weren't any custard creams, but he tried one of the cakes, and it was very nice, so he had two more.

'Is he OK eating those?' asked Misty Twiglet. 'Isn't all that sugar bad for him?'

'It doesn't seem to be,' said Daisy. 'He likes biscuits best.'

'Custard creams,' explained Kevin, through a big mouthful of cake.

'How interesting,' said Misty. 'Daisy, you must give me a list of all the things he likes to eat. Do have a cake!'

Daisy didn't understand why Misty would want a list of Kevin's favourite food, but she was too shy to say so. She took a chocolate eclair from the plate of cakes the pop star proffered, but she squeezed it a bit too hard and all the cream shot out and landed with a loud gloop on the polished floor near the fireplace. Luckily, Misty didn't notice. She saw Daisy looking worriedly towards the fireplace, but thought she was admiring the secret passage.

'Isn't it great?' Misty said. 'Like something in a spooky old story! It's ever

so narrow—just room in places to squeeze
through. It comes out through a little
green door in the undergrowth behind
the church in Little Strimming. I love it!
When I was your age I lived in a boring,
modern flat, and I always wished I could
have a big old mysterious house like this,
with secret passages and panelled walls and
suits of armour standing about and doors
with proper keyhole-shaped keyholes that
you could actually spy through. And the
gardens are going to be filled with all sorts
of quaint creatures, it'll be just perfect!'

'Er, Misty . . .' said Baz Gumption,
tapping his watch.

'Oh dear!' Misty took Daisy's hands and
smiled sorrowfully at her. 'I have to go!
I'm due in the big city to record a charity

single for the *Let's Stamp Out Athlete's Foot* campaign. Baz, can you make sure Daisy gets home safely? And thank you SO MUCH, Daisy!'

'Mmpff,' said Daisy. She realized that her meeting with Misty was almost at an end. It was the most important thing that had ever happened to her, and she hadn't been able to think of anything to say, and she wouldn't even have anything to prove that the whole visit hadn't been a dream, because she was much too shy to ask for a selfie. 'Please may I—' she stammered,

'May I have your autograph?'

'Of course!' said Misty sweetly. 'And I should have your autograph, too!' (She was used to talking to tongue-tied fans, and she found that asking them for *their* autographs helped to put them at their ease.) Quick as a flash, Baz Gumption produced a pink pen and two pieces of paper. Misty wrote on one of them,

To my good friend Daisy – thanks for bringing Kevin over!

Misty Twiglet xxx

On the second piece Daisy carefully wrote her own name in her very best handwriting. Then Misty jumped up, hugged Daisy, and hurried outside, where Lumphammer the butler had loaded all the suitcases and hatboxes into the big black car, and a chauffeur was waiting to drive Misty to the big city.

As Misty stepped outside a strange sound came drifting across the twilit garden. 'AOoooEEEfoooOQoo!' it went. It sounded like someone playing a small, out-of-tune trombone underwater.

'Whatever's that?' asked Misty.

'That's just another one of the creatures I've found to stock your garden,' Baz Gumption said. 'Now hurry up, you don't want to be late.'

Daisy and Kevin stood in the doorway and watched as the car drove off, with Misty waving at them from the back window.

'I'll get Lumphammer to drive you home,' said Baz Gumption.

'Thank you,' said Daisy politely. 'But I can fly home on Kevin. He wouldn't fit in a car anyway.'

'Oh, but Kevin's staying here,' said Baz Gumption.

He held up the piece of paper where Daisy had written her autograph. She hadn't really looked at it when she was signing, because she had been concentrating too hard on writing her name clearly and neatly for Misty Twiglet. Now she saw that the paper was covered with printed words, with her signature right at the bottom.

'This here,' said Baz Gumption, 'is a contract, handing over control of that fat, flying pony to Baz Gumption Enterprises

Inc. He's not yours any more, little dudette. That pony is staying right here.'

'But—but—but . . .' burbled Daisy.

'Come on,' neighed Kevin, 'Let's go home!'

'Lumphammer!' yelled Baz Gumption. 'Grab that pony before he can get away!'

The butler came running. Before Daisy could jump onto Kevin's back Lumphammer looped a halter over Kevin's nose. Kevin flapped his wings and took off, but the halter was attached to a long, thick rope, and Lumphammer held tight to the other end. However hard he flapped, Kevin could not escape.

'Take him to his new home,' said Baz. 'I can drive Daisy back to Bumbleford myself.'

FOUR

KEVIN AND THE MONSTERS

Lumphammer the butler dragged Kevin away from the house on the end of his rope as if he was nothing but a big, white, pony-shaped balloon. Kevin struggled to break free, but after a while he realized that it was useless and just followed where Lumphammer led. He can't hold on to the rope forever, Kevin told himself. Sooner or later he'll let go, and then I'll fly away.

It was starting to get dark as they

walked through the woods beside the lake. Across the water came the same eerie noise that Kevin had heard earlier, but it sounded much louder and nearer now. **'AWoOOOAAAIEEE!'** it went. It made all the hairs in Kevin's mane stand up on end. 'What's that?' he asked.

"Oo knows?' said Lumphammer. 'There's all sorts of beasties living here now. Baz is filling the place with monsters and weirdos like you.'

Kevin was offended. He wasn't a weirdo! He was a beautiful, magic, flying pony! He certainly didn't belong in a place full of monsters. He'd never met a monster, but he thought they were probably scary and mean. Those eerie, screeching noises were still coming

from the lake, and they made him wish
he was back in his own nest, nibbling
a custard cream and getting ready to
snuggle down for the night.

Beyond the lake there was a sort of
rocky crag, and on the far side of the
crag there was a section of the garden
which had been sealed off with a high
fence. Lumphammer went to a gate in the
fence, pushed it open, and pulled Kevin
through. 'This here is your enclosure,' said
Lumphammer. 'Welcome to your new 'ome.'

Ha! thought Kevin to himself, as the
beastly butler detached the rope from his
halter and went back out through the gate.
I won't be staying here for long! What
a twit! Has he forgotten I'm a FLYING
pony? He flapped his wings as hard as

they would flap and went zooming up into the sky—but he hadn't gone far before something stopped him. A net had been fixed over the top of the enclosure like a see-through roof. It was so thin that Kevin hadn't noticed it until he flew into it, and so strong that he could not push through. 'Argh! Blap! Snargle!' said Kevin, tumbling back to the ground.

'Nighty night!' said Lumphammer, and he locked the gate and walked away through the woods, whistling.

Kevin looked around the enclosure. There was a manger in one corner, but it was full of hay, not custard creams. There was a smart little stable, but Kevin had never slept in a stable. He felt awfully homesick. He missed his nest, and he missed Max and Daisy. Two tears trickled down his nose and dripped off the end. Plop, plop.

Sadly, he started dragging the straw outside to make a nest, and wondered how long he would have to stay in this nasty place. He was sure Max and Daisy's mum and dad would sort things out when they heard what had happened. He hoped it would be soon.

He had just finished the nest and settled down in it when a dry twig snapped somewhere on the far side of the fence. Kevin raised his head and looked around. He had forgotten about the monsters, but there they were—shadowy shapes, emerging from the trees. The moonlight made silvery reflections in their eyes.

'GO AWAY, MONSTERS!' Kevin shouted.

'We're not monsters,' said the monsters.

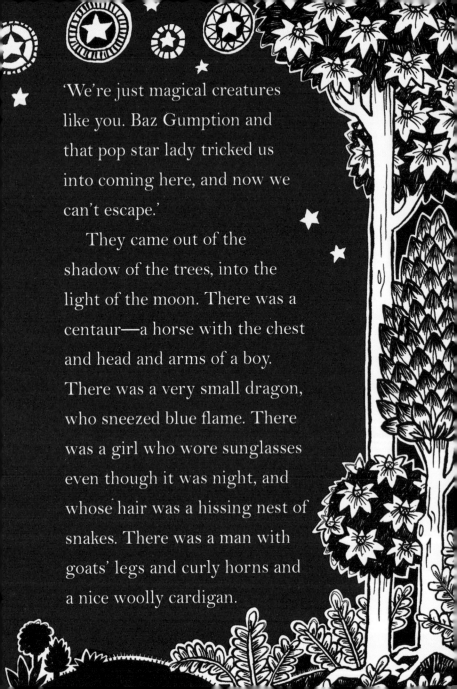

'We're just magical creatures like you. Baz Gumption and that pop star lady tricked us into coming here, and now we can't escape.'

They came out of the shadow of the trees, into the light of the moon. There was a centaur—a horse with the chest and head and arms of a boy. There was a very small dragon, who sneezed blue flame. There was a girl who wore sunglasses even though it was night, and whose hair was a hissing nest of snakes. There was a man with goats' legs and curly horns and a nice woolly cardigan.

I see what Lumphammer meant, thought Kevin. What a bunch of weirdos! But it did make him feel a bit happier knowing that he wasn't the only prisoner of Gloomsbury Grange. He drew himself up proudly, raised his wings, and said, 'I'm KEVIN. Never fear, I'll get you out of here.'

FIVE

MAX MAKES A PLAN

Max's swimming competition had gone
really well. He almost won one race,
and his team would have won the relay
too, except that Ellie Fidgett was upset
because her guinea pigs had vanished
again and it made her swim more slowly
than usual. (The guinea pigs' names were
Neville and Beyoncé. They had floated
away on their hutch during the Great
Bumbleford Flood and it had given them a
taste for adventure. They were ALWAYS

getting lost.)

After the competition Mum and Dad took Max for pizza, and by the time they got home Daisy was already asleep—at least, the light in her room was off and there was a note on her door which said

GO AWAY
I'M ASLEEP.
LEAVE ME ALONE!!

Max wanted to run up to the roof and show Kevin the silver medal he'd won, even though Dad said it probably wasn't real silver. But Mum said Kevin would be asleep too, and Max should go to bed and tell him all about the swimming in the morning.

The next morning, Mum and Dad both had to go to work. Mum peeped into Max's room before she left and said, 'Be nice to Daisy today. I think she might be coming down with a cold or something— she's awfully grumpy, and she didn't want her breakfast. You know where I am if you need me!'

When she had gone, Max got out of bed and went to the kitchen. Daisy was sitting there looking glum. He said 'Hello', but she didn't reply. She didn't say anything while he ate his bowl of cereal and drank some juice, but when he said, 'Right, I'm going to go and show Kevin my swimming medal,' she shouted, 'NO!'

'I mean . . . he might not be awake yet,' she added.

'I'll wake him up then. It's nearly half past nine,' said Max.

'You might get wet.'

'It isn't raining.'

'But it might start.'

'It's a lovely sunny day! I'm going to show Kevin my medal, and then we'll go for a quick fly.'

'You can't,' said Daisy.

Max was confused. 'Why not?'

'BECAUSE KEVIN'S GONE! ALL RIGHT? BECAUSE I TOOK HIM TO SEE MISTY TWIGLET AND SHE WAS REALLY NICE AND SHE MADE ME SIGN AN AUTOGRAPH

FOR HER ONLY IT WASN'T AN AUTOGRAPH IT WAS A CONTRACT AND NOW KEVIN BELONGS TO HER AND HE'S LIVING AT GLOOMSBURY GRANGE IN A SPECIAL CAGE AND I FEEL AWWWWWFFFFUUUUULLL!' wailed Daisy.

Max ran out of the flat and up the stairs to the roof. Kevin's nest was empty. Max ran back down. Daisy had gone into her room. He ignored the KEEP OUT notices and pushed the door open. Daisy was lying on her bed. She had torn down all her posters of Misty Twiglet and ripped them into little bits. They lay strewn on the carpet like gloomy confetti at a goth's wedding.

'She seemed SO NICE,' Daisy sniffled. 'But she just wanted Kevin, and she TRICKED me into signing that rotten contract, and I HATE her. I always thought it would be wonderful and romantic to have a broken heart and live out my days in sorrow, but now I really actually have a broken heart and it feels HORRID.'

Max felt sorry for her. 'I don't think kids CAN sign contracts,' he said. 'I don't think it counts unless you're a grown-up. I'm going to call Mum and she'll take us to Gloomsbury Grange and ask them to let Kevin go.' He ran to the living room and started dialling the number for Bubblecutz, Mum's underwater hairdressing salon.

'NO!' shouted Daisy, running after

him. 'PLEASE don't tell Mum! I've been SO STUPID. She'll be really cross with me! Or maybe she'll be all kind and understanding and that will be WORSE.'

'But she'll find out anyway,' said Max. 'When she gets home tonight and Kevin isn't here . . . Unless we could get him back before that.'

'But how?' sniffled Daisy.

'We could get a bus out to Gloomsbury Grange and ask them to give Kevin back.'

'They'll say no! There's this butler called Lumphammer and he's really big and scary! He's like a troll or something!'

Max thought for a moment. 'OK, we won't ask. We'll just sneak into the gardens and free Kevin.'

'But how can we sneak in? There are

great big gates, and a really high wall!'

'Hmm,' said Max, frowning. 'And there's no other way in at all?'

'No,' said Daisy. Then she remembered something. 'Yes!' she said. 'There's a secret passage! Misty showed it to me. It's in the wall beside the fireplace. And she said the other end is at Little Strimming . . .' She tried to remember what Misty had told her. 'She said there's a green door near the church . . .'

'BRILLIANT!' said Max, and he ran to get a torch, because he thought secret passages were probably a bit on the shady side. He put it in his rucksack, along with some other things he thought might come in handy on a rescue mission:

1. PLENTY OF BISCUITS

2. PICNIC BLANKET (TARTAN)

3. STICKY TAPE

4. SOME WIRE CUTTERS FROM DAD'S TOOL BOX

5. WATER

6. EMERGENCY
BACK-UP BISCUITS

'We'll sneak in, rescue Kevin, and fly home on him! Mum and Dad will never know he was gone, and I bet Misty Twiglet will never have the nerve to ask for him back!'

Daisy wiped her eyes on her hankie, realized it was an official Misty Twiglet hankie, and threw it in the bin. She smiled a slightly hopeful smile.

'TO GLOOMSBURY GRANGE!' yelled Max.

SIX

TO THE RESCUE!

One quick bus ride to Little Strimming
later, Max and Daisy were hunting around
in the weeds at the back of the churchyard.
The churchyard was so overgrown that
it looked a bit like one of Misty Twiglet's
album covers, except that it wasn't foggy
and the sun was shining and there weren't
any dancing ghosts. It took Max and Daisy
about twenty minutes to find the green door
which led into the secret passage.

Max was afraid that it would be locked, but it wasn't. Maybe because it was a secret door, and so thickly overgrown with bushes, there wasn't any need to lock it. Or maybe the lock had just fallen off, because it was a very old door. When they pushed it open it creaked like the door of a haunted house in a scary film. The passage inside was dark and narrow, and smelled a bit like cabbage.

'There might be spiders,' said Max, as he shone his torch at the cobwebby ceiling.

'There might be rats,' said Daisy, as he shone it at the dusty floor.

But they were here to rescue their friend, and they were not going to be driven back by dust and cobwebs and a cabbagey smell. They set off down the passage. Daisy stomped along as loudly as she could to

scare rats away, and Max pulled his hood
up in case her stomping dislodged anything
with too many legs from the ceiling.
The passage led them under the walls of
Gloomsbury Grange and up a long and
winding stairway to the secret door in the
panelling beside Misty
Twiglet's fireplace.

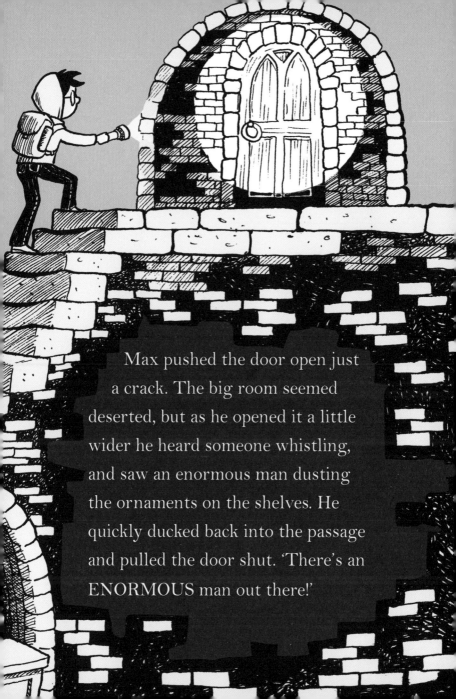

Max pushed the door open just a crack. The big room seemed deserted, but as he opened it a little wider he heard someone whistling, and saw an enormous man dusting the ornaments on the shelves. He quickly ducked back into the passage and pulled the door shut. 'There's an ENORMOUS man out there!'

'Is he wearing a black suit, like a butler?'

'Yes, but he's put a pink flowery pinafore over it 'cos he's doing some dusting.'

'That must be Lumphammer. I said he was big and scary.'

'Yes,' said Max, 'but you didn't say HOW big and scary. You said he was like a troll, but he's more like a . . .' he tried to think of something bigger and scarier than a troll. 'A P.E. teacher or something!'

'Shhh!' said Daisy. The whistling was coming closer. They heard the feathers of Lumphammer's duster whisk across the panelling a few inches from their hiding place. They crouched in the dark, trying not to make a sound.

WHISTLE WHISTLE. *WHISK*
WHISK WHISK. WHISTLE WHISTLE.
WHISK WHISK WHISK . . .

Then the whistling and the whisking slowly faded, and at last all was quiet. Max pushed the door open again, and checked that the butler had gone. Then he and Daisy scampered across the room, opened the French windows, and ran out into the gardens.

They didn't know where they were going, but they had to go somewhere, because there was a swimming pool just behind the house and floating about in it on an inflatable armchair was Baz Gumption. He was talking loudly into his mobile phone. 'Yes, Misty, of course I've got the fat, flying pony safe. Now we really need to find some unicorns. No collection of mythical creatures is complete without some unicorns . . .' He hadn't seen Max and Daisy, but they knew he would if he turned around, so they fled as quickly as they could across the lawn and into the deep shadows of the trees.

All at once, a strange creature barred their way. He looked like a man, but he had big curly horns growing out of his hair, and his legs were furry and ended in little hoofs. His eyes were the colour of sunlight in autumn woods.

'Hello!' said Max. 'That's a nice cardigan!'

'Why thank you,' said the creature, looking pleased. 'I am Cardigan Faun. Most fauns come from places like Ancient Greece where it's nice and warm, but my family lives in the wild, wet hills of the Outermost West where it can get a bit chilly, so we're all into knitwear in a big way. I knitted this cardigan myself. It has Extra Pockets. Your friend Kevin sent me to keep watch for you, by the way. He was sure you would come to rescue him.'

'Can you take us to him?' asked Daisy.

'Of course!' said Cardigan Faun, and trotted off so quickly that Max and Daisy had to run to keep up. The path led along the shore of the lake, and as they hurried

along it a strange sound came from the
water—'OWEEEO°°°AAEIIEEE!'
it went, only worse.

'That's the weird noise we heard last
night!' said Daisy.

'What is it?' Max asked nervously.

'Oh, that's just the mermaid,' said
Cardigan Faun. He stopped by the water's
edge and shouted, 'Oi! Iris! Put a sock in it!'

A mermaid with pointy spectacles bobbed to the surface and threw a fish at him. 'How rude!' she said. 'I'm just singing my eerie, haunting songs, like a mermaid is supposed to.'

'Is that what you call it?' asked Cardigan Faun. 'It sounded like someone playing the tuba in an echo chamber. Oof!' he added, as another fish bounced off his face.

'Welcome to Gloomsbury Grange,' said Iris, doing a sort of watery curtsey to Max and Daisy. 'How did Baz Gumption trick you into joining this miserable menagerie? He told me I'd have my own private island and plenty of cake, but the island's just a very hard rock in the middle of this pond, and the cake is all shop-bought. I suppose they're going to keep me here forever, and that won't do—I'd arranged to meet my friends Oliver and Cliff in Farsight Cove next week so we can go and watch the annual Underwater Fireworks Display, the most glamorous and technically challenging event in the whole mermaid social calendar. They'll be awfully worried if I don't show up. What are you two meant to be anyway? You don't look very mythical.'

'They aren't!' said Cardigan Faun. 'This is Max and Daisy. They've come to rescue the little flying pony who arrived last night.'

'Lucky for some,' said Iris, and submerged again. Bubbles came to the surface where she had been, and popped to let out more of her strange song. 'Oooh... EEEEH... AAAAH ...POM-TE-TIDDLE-TE-POM...'

'So how many creatures is Misty Twiglet keeping prisoner here?' asked Max.

'There are five of us,' said the faun. 'Six if you count your friend Kevin. That Baz Gumption tricked us all here with one promise or another. Take me, for example. Baz told me that Misty was launching her own range of cardigans and wanted to use

me as a model, but she never did, and
I've been stuck here ever since.'

THE FRASER HUTCH

THE HOXTON

THE STUART PILE

'When we've got Kevin out,' said Max,
'we'll see if we can help you too.'

'I'm going to write a VERY strongly
worded letter of complaint to the Misty
Twiglet Fan Club,' said Daisy.

'I don't suppose it will do any good,'

sighed Cardigan Faun glumly. 'Nobody will
believe that a pop sensation would send
her manager and butler around kidnapping
fauns and mermaids and dragons. Most
people don't even believe there are any such
things as fauns and mermaids and dragons,
which doesn't help. Ah, here we are! And
here's your friend.'

They had come to an enclosure at the
foot of a rocky crag. There, looking out at
them through the links of the fence,
was Kevin.

'Kevin!' shouted Max, and reached through the wire to scratch the pony's nose and give him some of the custard creams which he had brought all the way from Bumbleford and bravely not eaten on the journey. Then he rummaged in his rucksack and took out the wire-cutters. **PLINK! PLINK! PLINNNNN-K** . . .

The wire strands were tough and took a lot of cutting, but Daisy took over when

Max got tired, and before long they had cut a Kevin-sized hole in the fence. Kevin squeezed through it.

'Come on!' shouted Max. 'Let's fly out of here!'

Kevin let Max and Daisy hug him, and licked their faces. He was SO glad to see them, and so pleased to think that he would soon be back in his own nest on the roof of their flat. They climbed onto his back and he got ready to take off. But then he saw Cardigan Faun waving him a sad goodbye, and he thought about the other creatures he would be leaving behind. It wouldn't be fair to escape without them, however badly he might want to.

Once again, two tears rolled down his nose. Plop, plop.

'What's wrong, Kevin?' asked Max, jumping down off Kevin's back again. 'Are you still weak from lack of biscuits?'

'Are your wings hurt?' asked Daisy.

But Kevin's wings were fine, and he wasn't in any more need of biscuits than usual. Max and Daisy turned round. Watching them from the shadows at the edge of the wood were Cardigan Faun, a centaur, a gorgon, and a very small dragon.

'I can't go without my friends,' said Kevin.

SEVEN
PRISONERS OF GLOOMSBURY GRANGE

Max opened one of the packets of biscuits
he had brought, and offered them round.
The mythical creatures each took one, and
introduced themselves. The gorgon's name
was Zola, the centaur was called Cedric,
and the little dragon's name was Belling.
Max and Daisy were a bit worried about
looking at Zola to start with, because they
remembered hearing that looking at a

gorgon would turn you to stone, but Zola said that was just a made-up story. 'Those bloomin' Greek Myths got it the wrong way round,' she said. 'It's me looking at you that turns you to stone. And it only works if I take my sunglasses off and really glare at you. We gorgons call it "giving someone a Hard Stare", that's a sort of gorgon joke. Only I'm not very good at it. I was bottom of my class at Miss Medusa's Academy. All my friends used to tease me about it. Even the snakes on their heads used to snigger at

me in a hissy kind of way. That's why I
went wandering off on my own, and Baz
and Lumphammer caught me and brought
me here.'

'I was out for a nice gallop in the woods
when they captured me,' said Cedric the
centaur sadly. 'There was a van parked in a
glade with a sign saying "Free Oatcakes"!
I'd never heard of oatcakes, but they
sounded great! Oats and a cake—that's a
centaur's dream come
true! So I trotted
into the back of the
van, and Baz and
Lumphammer
slammed the door
shut and drove
me here!'

Belling the dragon and Cardigan Faun
nodded sadly. They had similar stories to tell.

'It was firelighters in the van when
I saw it,' said Belling. 'Mmm,
yummy, yummy
firelighters . . .'

'And we SO want to go home!' sniffled
Cardigan Faun. 'I left my family up in
the wild, wet hills and I can't even get
a message to them—the signal here is
rubbish.' He pulled a mobile phone from
one of his cardigan pockets and showed
them a picture of his wife and children,
who were all wearing neat little cardigans
of their own.

Zola started to cry too. So did all her snakes. Cedric the centaur brushed away a tear. Belling gave a sad little sneeze and blue flames flickered from his nostrils, like the pilot light of the boiler in Max and Daisy's flat.

'Well,' said Daisy, 'I'm SHOCKED that Misty Twiglet would send her rotten henchmen out to kidnap unsuspecting mythical animals and imprison them in her garden. She's officially no longer my favourite pop star.'

'Don't worry,' Max told the miserable mythical creatures. 'We're going to get you all out of here.'

But how? He looked at them all. Kevin could fly out over the wall, and if he made extra trips he could probably carry Cardigan Faun and Zola, but he couldn't carry Cedric. And what about Iris the mermaid? She would just slide off Kevin's back!

'We'll have to get you out the same way we came in, through the secret passage,' said Max.

'But Lumphammer and Baz are at the house!' said Daisy. 'They're bound to notice if we try sneaking a load of mythical creatures past them. That's exactly the sort of thing they'll be looking out for!'

'Maybe Zola could turn them to stone?' suggested Max.

The young gorgon blushed. 'I don't think I could,' she said. 'I wasn't being modest when I said I'm not good at Hard Stares. The people I turn to stone all seem to turn right back into people again after about ten seconds.'

'Ten seconds isn't nearly long enough to get us all into the secret passage,' said Daisy.

'Then we'll have to cause a distraction somehow,' said Max. 'I know! You fly out over the wall on Kevin, and ring the bell

on the big gates at the end of the drive.
Baz and Lumphammer will go to see
who it is, and you can keep them talking
while the rest of us creep into the secret
passage.'

'But what will I keep them talking
ABOUT?' complained Daisy. 'They'll know
who I am! They'll just say, "go away"!'

Everyone looked glum. Then Kevin had
an idea. 'You could be in DISGUISE!'
he said.

'But what sort of disguise?'
wondered Max.

'A custard cream!' suggested Kevin. He had seen someone dressed up as a giant biscuit on Bumbleford High Street once to advertise a new café and he had thought they looked very convincing and memorable. He would be very distracted if a giant biscuit came ringing on his doorbell.

But Daisy and Max didn't seem too keen on his idea, and anyway, there was nothing in Misty Twiglet's garden that could be used to make a giant custard cream costume, or even a rich tea finger.

Just then, something rustled in the bushes nearby. Everyone looked round, afraid that Baz or Lumphammer had come to check on them. But out of the bushes wandered two guinea pigs.

'It's Neville and Beyoncé!' said Daisy.

'Ellie Fidgett's been looking everywhere for them!' said Max, and he ran happily over to the guinea pigs and picked them up.

They had given him a Brilliant Idea.

EIGHT

THE DOOR-TO-DOOR UNICORN SELLER

Baz Gumption was still drifting on his
inflatable chair in the swimming pool.
He was enjoying lazing about at Misty's
posh house while she was away. He didn't
notice Kevin rise out of the woods behind
the house with Daisy and Cardigan Faun
on his back and fly out over the wall. Baz
was far too busy playing a game called
KITTENS KROSSING on his phone.

In the game you had to help a cutesy
kitten cross a busy road without it getting
squashed by any of the cars or lorries,
but Baz liked making the cars and lorries
swerve to run over the cutesy kittens; that
was just the sort of person he was.

DING-DONG went a noise. It was the
sound of the bell on the main gate.

'Lumphammer, go and see who that is,'
yelled Baz, without looking up from his game.

'Aww, boss, I just got changed!' moaned
Lumphammer, coming out of the house
in a pair of bright blue swimming trunks.
He had finished the housework and was
looking forward to a nice swim. 'I can't go
down to the gate in my swimmers!' he said.

'You don't need to, big dude,' said Baz.

'Just use the intercom in the kitchen.
See who's ringing the bell, and tell them
to go away. I'm extremely busy with
important work.'

MIAOW-VROOM-SPLAT

went his phone.

Lumphammer
stomped back
into the house. He
pressed the button on
the intercom and said,
"Oo's there?'

'Do you want to buy some unicorns?' said a nervous little crackly voice. 'I've got a pair of lovely unicorns for sale. I heard your boss was looking for unicorns.'

'Ooh,' said Lumphammer. 'Hold on!'

He trudged back outside. 'Baz, it's someone selling unicorns!'

Baz was so surprised that he accidentally let a cute kitten get all the way across the road. 'A door-to-door unicorn seller! What a stroke of luck!' He paddled his inflatable chair to the poolside and scrambled out. 'You wait here, Lumphammer,' he said, putting on a dressing gown over his swimming trunks. 'I'll go and have a word.'

In the shrubbery beyond the pool, Max,

Zola the gorgon, Cedric the centaur, Belling the dragon, and Iris the mermaid watched him go. 'Yes!' they said, as he hurried off. And then, 'No!', because Lumphammer stayed right where he was, and they knew there was no way they could get into the house without him seeing them.

'Ooh, ow, ouch!' grumbled Baz Gumption, as he strode towards the gates. He had forgotten to put his flip-flops on, and the gravel drive was hurting his feet, but he was so eager to see the unicorns that he didn't care.

The door-to-door unicorn seller was an odd-looking person. A very tall lady, wearing big black sunglasses, a woolly cardigan, and a long tartan skirt. (Pssst! She wasn't REALLY a door-to-door unicorn seller, of course. As you've probably guessed, she was actually Daisy, wearing Cardigan Faun's cardigan and sitting on Cardigan Faun's shoulders, with a picnic blanket wrapped around Cardigan Faun like a skirt.) In each hand she held a small, hairy animal.

'Would you be interested in buying two unicorns at all?' she asked.

(Pssst! The unicorns weren't REALLY unicorns, of course. As you've probably guessed, they were actually Neville and Beyoncé. Max had borrowed two pointy

seashells from Iris the Mermaid's hairdo
and stuck them to the guinea pigs'
foreheads with sticky tape to make them
LOOK like unicorns. But they still didn't
look much like unicorns.)

'They don't look much like unicorns,' said Baz, peering at them through the bars of the gate. 'I thought they'd be taller. And more sort of *horsey*, if you know what I mean.'

'These are South American Long-Haired Miniature Unicorns,' said Daisy. 'They're extra rare. I'm a well-known South American Long-Haired Miniature Unicorn breeder. My name is . . . Er . . .'

Daisy hadn't thought of a fake name

for herself yet. She quickly looked around for inspiration. Mrs Gates? Too obvious. Mrs Cardigan? That didn't sound like a real name. 'Letterbox!' she said. 'Mrs Letterbox. Perhaps you've heard of me?'

'Hmmmm,' said Baz Gumption.

Kevin watched from his hiding place in some nearby bushes. He wondered how Max and the others were getting on. They should be about halfway along the secret passage by now . . .

ɔ∪ɕ

But Max and the others were still hiding in the shrubbery, watching while Lumphammer stood on the side of the swimming pool and tried to work up the courage to dive in.

'Well, we can't get into the house without that big lunk seeing us,' said Iris. 'We'd better call off this whole half-baked escape plan.' (She was in a bad mood because the only way the others could think of to get her through the secret passage was in a wheelbarrow which they had found in the potting shed. Max had filled it with water, but Iris thought being wheeled about in a wheelbarrow was very undignified.)

'No,' said Max. He turned to Zola. 'I bet you're a much better gorgon than you think you are, Zola. I don't care what those bullies at your school say. I bet you can turn Lumphammer into stone with one of your Hard Stares. Just for long enough to let us get past him into the house.'

'No, I can't,' said the gorgon. 'I've never managed to turn anyone into stone for more than a few seconds . . .'

'You can do it!' said Max, and all the others agreed. Unfortunately, they agreed so loudly that Lumphammer heard them.

''Oo's that?' he grunted. ''Oo's hidin' in that there shrubbery?'

NINE

THE GREAT ESCAPE

As Lumphammer started lumbering around the edge of the pool to find out what the noises were, Max shoved Zola out of the shrubbery.

'Oi! You get back to the gorgon enclosure RIGHT NOW!' roared Lumphammer. 'Or I'll have your snakes for garters!'

Zola stared hard at the oncoming butler. 'It's not working!' she squeaked.

Lumphammer reached down and clutched his leg. 'Ooh, I've gone a bit stiff . . .'

'It IS working!' said Max. 'Stare harder, Zola!'

So Zola glared and glared, and slowly the colour seemed to drain out of Lumphammer, and his movements grew slower and slower until there was just a statue of him standing there beside the pool. 'Mmmff gmmmff mmmfff bmmff mpfff!' the statue said, but not loudly enough for anyone to hear.

Max cheered. He jumped out of the shrubbery and raced around the swimming pool and into the house, with Zola and Belling following close behind, and Cedric the Centaur wheeling Iris along in her barrow.

Meanwhile, down at the gates, Baz
Gumption had decided that South American
Long-Haired Miniature Unicorns were
better than no unicorns at all.

'Well, Mrs Letterbox, what price are you
asking for these two unicorns of yours?'

'Ten pounds!' said Daisy.

'Atchoo!' said her tummy.

'What was that?' asked Baz.

'Nothing!' said Daisy.

'Ahhhh-CHOO!' said her tummy again.

Poor Cardigan Faun! His head was
hidden inside his own cardigan, and the
woolly fibres were tickling his nose.
'AHHH-CHOOO!' he sneezed, so hard that
a button popped off the cardigan and hit
Baz Gumption in the face.

'Wait a minute!' shouted Baz Gumption.

'You're not a door-to-door unicorn seller at all! You're just trying to distract my attention for some reason!'

Cardigan Faun sneezed again. This time Daisy toppled off his shoulders, and her too-big sunglasses fell off.

'You!' growled Baz. 'And YOU!' he gasped, recognizing Cardigan Faun. He turned and started sprinting back up the drive, shouting, 'Oooh, ow, Lumphammer!

The—ouch, oogh—weirdoes are escaping!'

But there was nothing Lumphammer could do about it. Zola the gorgon had really given him the works, and he was still standing motionless beside the pool. Baz didn't even recognize him when he came running round to the back of the house and crashed into him. 'Oww!' he shouted. 'Lumphammer! Why have you left this stupid ugly statue here? Where are you? There's a flippin' ESCAPE going on! We need to round up those creatures before any more get away . . .'

Then he noticed a wet tyre
track leading across the patio, into
the house. He bent down and touched it.
'Hmmm. Looks like a wheelbarrow came
this way recently . . .'

WIBBLE!

'Mmgff mm ffmmf mgpmfff!' said
Lumphammer.

Baz finally recognized the statue.
'Lumphammer, you petrified poltroon!
Don't just stand there! Help me catch
them!'

The gorgon's Hard Stare was starting

SQUEAK!

to wear off. With a
great effort Lumphammer
swung his stony legs and
clumped along behind Baz.
Together they followed the tracks
of the wheelbarrow into Misty Twiglet's
living room. The wheel-print led to the
panelled wall beside the fireplace, where
it vanished.

'You know what this means!' growled
Baz.

'Yes!' said Lumphammer. 'Er . . . What?'

'They're using the secret passage!
Quick, get round the other end and cut
them off!'

'Right,' said Lumphammer, and started to

stomp v-e-r-y s-l-o-w-l-y towards the door.

'ARGH!' yelled Baz. 'All right, you stay here and guard this end and I'LL cut them off!'

Meanwhile, Max and the mythical creatures were making their way through the secret passage. They crept along it, with Belling the dragon breathing small yellow flames to light their way. Cedric the centaur was having trouble getting Iris's wheelbarrow down the long, winding staircase. Every time the barrow bumped down another step Iris said, 'Ow, watch it, you're spilling water everywhere!'

'Oh, do hurry!' whispered Max.

Outside the gate, Daisy had picked herself up and was dusting herself off, while Cardigan Faun carefully re-buttoned his cardigan. 'I just hope we kept Baz talking long enough for the others to reach the secret passage!' said Daisy. 'Kevin, can you fly us over to the churchyard so we can be there when they come out the other end?'

Kevin poked his head out of a bush, where he had found some quite interesting leaves to eat. 'That man's coming back,' he said.

Daisy looked round. Baz was pounding down the drive towards her. 'Ooh, argh, ow!' he shouted, as his bare feet crunched over the pointy gravel. He had the button which controlled the gates in his hand, and he pressed it as he ran so that the

gates were already swinging open when he
reached them. He grabbed Cardigan Faun
by the cardigan and threw him inside the
gates. Then he grabbed Daisy and threw
her after Cardigan Faun. 'I'll deal with you
two later!' he yelled, pressing the button
again. As the gates slammed shut, he

sprinted off towards the churchyard.

'Kevin, do something!' wailed Daisy. 'He'll catch Max and the others when they come out of the green door!'

Kevin finished his mouthful of leaves and took off. But he didn't know where the secret passage came out, and although he soared high into the air he couldn't see Baz, who was under the trees, running down the leafy path to the churchyard.

Kevin saw something else, though. He saw Misty Twiglet's big black car turning off the main road onto the lane which led to Little Strimming.

'Humf!' said Kevin. He flapped his wings, glided down towards the car, and landed on the road just in front of it.

Misty Twiglet stuck her head out of the car window. 'Hey, it's Kevin! What are you doing out here, Kevin?'

'Humpf!' said Kevin again. He stood squarely in the middle of the road so that the car couldn't pass. 'You are a BAD pop sensation!'

◡♌◡

'We're there!' said Max, as the escaping creatures reached the end of the passage and he saw sunlight peeping through the slats of the old door. But there was a surprise waiting for them when they opened the door and tumbled out into the

churchyard, and it wasn't a nice surprise,
like a load of presents, or a cake. It was
Baz Gumption.

'Ha!' he said. 'So you thought you could
outwit ME, did you?'

'Zola, give him a Hard Stare!'
Max yelled.

But Baz was ready for that.
He whipped a pair of mirror
sunglasses out of his
pocket and put them on.
'Bother!' said Zola, as
her stare bounced back at
her and she turned into
a statue of herself.

Belling the dragon took a deep breath and got ready to blow fire at Baz, but Baz pulled out a fire extinguisher and squirted it at him.

'Bleugh!' said Belling, breathing out a little cloud of steam, and he started to cry.

'Face it,' said Baz, 'you're all useless! You'd be much better safe in my garden.'

'It's not your garden,' said Max. 'It's Misty Twiglet's!'

'Pfff,' said Baz. 'Misty is FINISHED. She hasn't had a big hit for years! She's a has-been!

Nobody wants to hear songs about lonely ghosts any more! She's been trying to find an exciting new sound, but she's all out of ideas. She's on her way down, but she's not taking me with her. That's why I persuaded her to do this stupid charity single for Athlete's Foot. Once people associate her name with an itchy fungal infection of the toes her career will be well and truly finished. Then I'll buy this place from her at a bargain price and open it as the world's only Mythical Zoo. When people hear I've got a dragon, a centaur and a real, live flying pony on display they'll come flocking. And I've just acquired some very rare South American Long-Haired Miniature Unicorns, too! So, what will it be? Are you going to go back along that secret passage like good mythical zoo animals, or will I have to call for

Lumphammer to bring a
fork-lift truck and a cage to
take you home in?'

Just then, there was a whir of
wingbeats overhead.

'Kevin!' shouted Max, as the roly-poly
flying pony came fluttering heroically down
through the trees.

'Good,' said Baz. 'I'll take him, too.'

But Kevin was not alone. Misty Twiglet was perching on his back, and she did not look pleased. In fact, she seemed to have been crying—her mascara had run, so she looked like a sad badger.

'Baz Gumption!' she shouted. 'What on earth are you playing at? Kevin has told me everything!'

'Daisy helped,' said Kevin. (He didn't really know enough words to tell Misty everything that had been happening while she was gone, but Daisy and Cardigan Faun had shouted to her through the gate, and she had let them out so that they could help Kevin explain.)

'You said these mythical creatures would be happy living in my garden!' Misty went on. 'I thought they'd come to live there because they WANTED to! I didn't realize you'd KIDNAPPED them! I'd never have let you talk me into collecting mythical creatures if I'd known you meant keeping them as PRISONERS! How DARE you trick me into making Daisy sign that contract!'

'Misty!' said Baz, trying his shiny smile on her, but it didn't work; it flickered and went out like a torch with wet batteries. 'I wasn't expecting you back from the big city yet. Don't you have that charity single to record?'

'I changed my mind!' said Misty. 'I realized that becoming the new face of Athlete's Foot would be a really bad idea. And it's not your only bad idea, is it, Baz?' She looked at Max and all the mythical creatures. 'I am SO SORRY!' she told them. 'I had no idea what Baz was really up to. I've been so busy I haven't had time to visit Gloomsbury Grange, but I hope that's all going to change. I want to spend lots of time here and make it a proper home . . .'

'Huh!' said Baz. 'No chance of that! You

can't afford a place like this, Misty. Your career is over. Nobody wants to hear your stupid, boring songs any more!'

'They will!' said Misty. 'Because I've just worked out what my NEW SOUND is going to be!'

She shoved Baz out of her way, and it wasn't her fault that he tripped over and fell into a big old patch of stinging nettles.

'Iris,' she said, walking over to the mermaid's wheelbarrow, 'I heard your strange songs wafting across the lake the other night, and I just can't get them out of my head! I was humming them all the way to the big city.'

'Coo, er, gosh!' said Iris, blushing a bit. 'Really? Nobody seems to like my songs usually.'

'All they need is a bit of work,' said Misty encouragingly. 'Maybe add a bit of a beat. And a tune. And some words. Will you help me write my next album?'

'Of course!' said Iris.

'And I love what you've done with your hair!' said Misty. 'Is that a real crab? Maybe you can help me with my new look as well as my new sound! That is . . .' She hesitated, and looked terribly worried. 'If you can ever forgive me?'

The mythical creatures thought they could.

'Maybe they could ALL help!' said Max. 'People might be bored of songs

about ghosts, but I bet they haven't heard
songs about dragons and centaurs and
mermaids and gorgons . . .'

'And FLYING PONIES,' said Kevin.

'And—ooh, unicorns!' said Misty.

'They aren't real unicorns,' said Daisy,
who had just arrived with Cardigan Faun.

They had brought Neville and Beyoncé with them, in case the adventure-loving guinea pigs decided to get lost again. 'But Cardigan Faun can play guitar, and he'd love to help out! And so would . . .' But Daisy got a bit shy then, and her voice trailed off into a little mumble.

Kevin took a firm mouthful of Misty's coat sleeve and tugged. When the pop sensation looked at him he twitched his wing in Daisy's direction. 'Daisy wants to sing too,' he said.

'Well,' said Misty Twiglet, 'we'll have to see.'

TEN

KEVIN GOES POP

In the end, everybody got to sing. Misty
Twiglet unveiled her new look and sound
at a special open-air concert on Bumbleford
Common. She arrived just as it was getting
dark, flying down to the stage on the back
of Kevin, who wore special glittery make-
up for the occasion. 'These are some songs
from my brand new album HIT AND
MYTH,' she said, 'and my friends are going
to help me sing them!'

The music began. Cardigan Faun
played guitar, Zola the gorgon clattered
a tambourine, and Cedric the centaur
was a knockout on the maracas. Belling
the dragon did spectacular flame effects
during the loudest bits. Iris and some of her
mermaid friends perched on pretend rocks
to sing backing vocals. And who was that
small mermaid who sang along with them?
It wasn't a mermaid at all, of course, it was
Daisy. (She was wearing a fake tail because
she'd felt silly being the only backing
singer with legs.) The stage was decorated
with banners and greenery and a pair of
impressive statues. Or were they statues?
Every now and then they seemed to move
a bit, as if they were trying to edge off
the stage, but then Zola would lower her

sunglasses and give them
a Hard Stare and they would
stand still again for the next few
songs. They looked pretty grumpy,
those two statues, but nobody else did.
The audience was having a grand old time.
Everyone in Bumbleford had come, and so
had all Cardigan Faun's family, and a small
herd of centaurs who went, 'Wooo!' every
time Cedric rattled his maracas. Up in the
sky, just out of the reach of the stage lights,
huge shapes circled on black bat wings—
baby Belling's mum and dad had flown down
from their cave in the mountains to watch
him, and they were very proud of him.

'There are some very peculiar people
here,' said Max's dad.

'That's what happens when you live

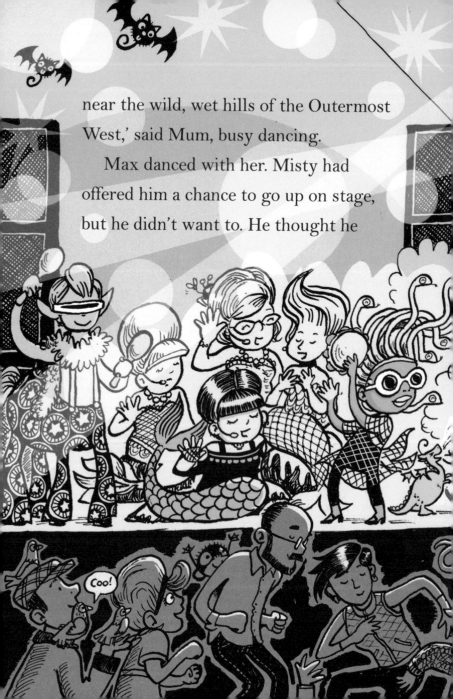

near the wild, wet hills of the Outermost West,' said Mum, busy dancing.

Max danced with her. Misty had offered him a chance to go up on stage, but he didn't want to. He thought he

Coo!

would enjoy the concert more if he was
in the crowd, and he was right.

After a while, Kevin came and found
him. Kevin had enjoyed being part of the
show, but it was quite loud on stage, and
the bright lights were a bit dazzling,
and he had decided that on the whole
he didn't want to be a pop star. So Max
climbed on to his wide back and they
flew up together to circle high above
the common, watching the dancing
and the lights and Belling's fireballs,
listening to the music echo away
across the town and out over
the river, where loads of Iris's

mermaid friends were looking on.
And what music it was, full of the
old magic of the western seas
and the wild, wet hills.

'So everything worked out all right!' Max said. 'Misty says we're all welcome to visit her at Gloomsbury Grange any time we like. She's going to fire Baz and Lumphammer as soon as they've finished being statues, and she's even making a big charity donation to the Stamp Out Athlete's Foot campaign, so everybody's happy!'

'Not Ellie Fidgett,' said Kevin.

There, below them, Ellie was making her way through the crowd. In the quiet bits between the songs Max could hear her shouting, 'Neville! Beyoncé! Where ARE you?'

'Those guinea pigs have only gone and got themselves lost AGAIN,' said Max. But he didn't feel too worried about them. This felt like a night for happy endings.

'I expect they'll turn up,' said Kevin.

And they did.

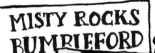

MISTY ROCKS
BUMBLEFORD

SARAH McINTYRE
LOVES PAPER
AND CHEWING
ON HER PENCILS.
SHE DRAWS
IN HER
STUDIO IN
LONDON AND LIVES IN A
NEIGHBOURHOOD WITH
TOWER BLOCKS LIKE THE
ONE WHERE MAX AND
DAISY LIVE.

ABOUT the AUTHORS

These two divas require many biscuits to produce their stories together. First they brainstorm ideas, and Philip asks Sarah what she would like to draw. Then Philip writes the words (with some help from Sarah) and Sarah draws the pictures (with some help from Philip).

PHILIP REEVE
LOVES
ESCAPING
THE CITY AND
ROAMING
AMONG THE
WILD, WET HILLS OF
DARTMOOR, WHICH
LOOKS VERY MUCH LIKE
THE OUTERMOST WEST.
HE OFTEN
ENCOUNTERS
ROLY-POLY PONIES.

MISTY TWIGLET
MYTH